I WANT TO BE AN
ENERGY ENGINEER

Written by
Jonathan Reule

Illustration
Carlos Varejão

Storyboard
Chong Wey Ming & Christiane Tee

First paperback edition October 2023
ISBN 978-981-17359-8-1

Published by Unibino Pte. Ltd.
9 North Buona Vista Drive, #02-01 Metropolis Tower 1, Singapore 138588

www.unibino.com

Energy is everywhere in our world. It's in the sunlight shining through the sky to the winds blowing across the lands. Energy exists in nearly everything. But using that energy to our advantage is an entire process in and of itself.

The next time you switch on the TV in your home or take a ride in a car or bus, know that these devices require energy to run. But how do we harness energy to power these machines? We can't throw a TV in a river and expect it to absorb the energy in that flowing stream. Nor can we leave our cars outside during a windy day, hoping that it will bring our vehicle to life, without the proper means to capture those sources of energy.

So how do we convert the energies in our natural world into electrical power? That's a good question and one that energy engineers could answer. You see, energy engineers are specialists who focus on how to harness energy from the world while storing that energy and eventually using it as a power supply.

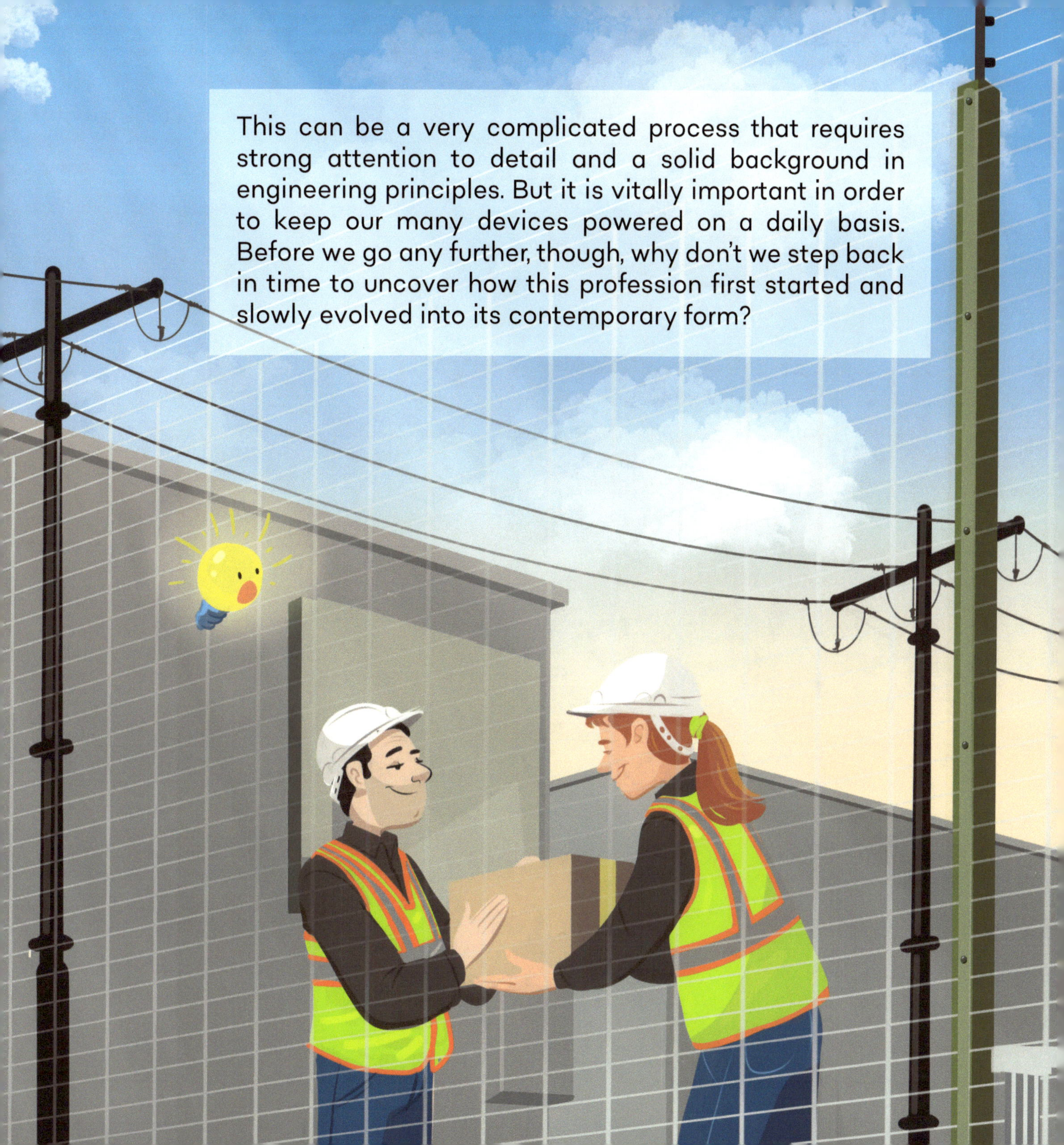
This can be a very complicated process that requires strong attention to detail and a solid background in engineering principles. But it is vitally important in order to keep our many devices powered on a daily basis. Before we go any further, though, why don't we step back in time to uncover how this profession first started and slowly evolved into its contemporary form?

First off, we've always used natural energy sources, even if we weren't able to store their power and convert them into electricity. For example, the sun has been one of our oldest and most reliable energy sources for ages. The sun not only gives us light during the day, but it also provides us with heat, especially during the months of summer.

But in those prehistoric times, we were limited by the sun's schedule for many tasks. When it came to hunting and farming, we often needed light to perform these daily chores, which kept us bound to the sun's rhythms. That is until we discovered how to build fires, which ended up being one of our first manmade energy sources.

For years, fires were a versatile source of energy that served many functions in our daily lives. They provided heat and light and helped us cook food and manufacture tools. But fires were not the only ancient energy source we could harness. As we built boats and learned to navigate rivers, we also discovered the power of moving water and how it allowed us to use less energy when rowing.

However, these early attempts at harnessing natural energy were limited by our technology. To fully utilise the energy available in our world, we needed to design better inventions and develop more sophisticated techniques for capturing and storing energy.

And that's exactly what the ancient Romans did in their cities thousands of years ago. They created one of the first technical watermills back in 25 BC to help with their daily chores. By using the power of a flowing water source, these watermills could be powered for a seemingly endless amount of time.

These early watermills
were often used to help grind
flour, chop wood, and even saw
stones in half. This wasn't the only way
the ancient Romans used natural energy
to their advantage, though. They also used
solar energy to help heat their bathhouses
by placing windows in the right areas to absorb
the most sunlight possible into the pools.

If we jump ahead to the medieval period in Iran, we will find similar technology, but this time a device that uses wind instead of water. Back in 700 AD, the Persian city of Sistan created what is known as Panemone windmills, which could be used in a similar fashion to watermills. What's even more impressive is that these Panemone windmills are still around and rotating to this day! These windmills were made with wood and designed in such a way that they can spin round and round as long as there is a breeze!

Just like the ancient watermills, these Panemone windmills were also used for grinding corn and pumping water. Yet, they had another purpose different from the watermill - protecting the city from storms. How did they do that, you might ask? Well, these windmills were built atop a hill and spread over a large expanse of area, making them a great buffer for pesky storms and the city below.

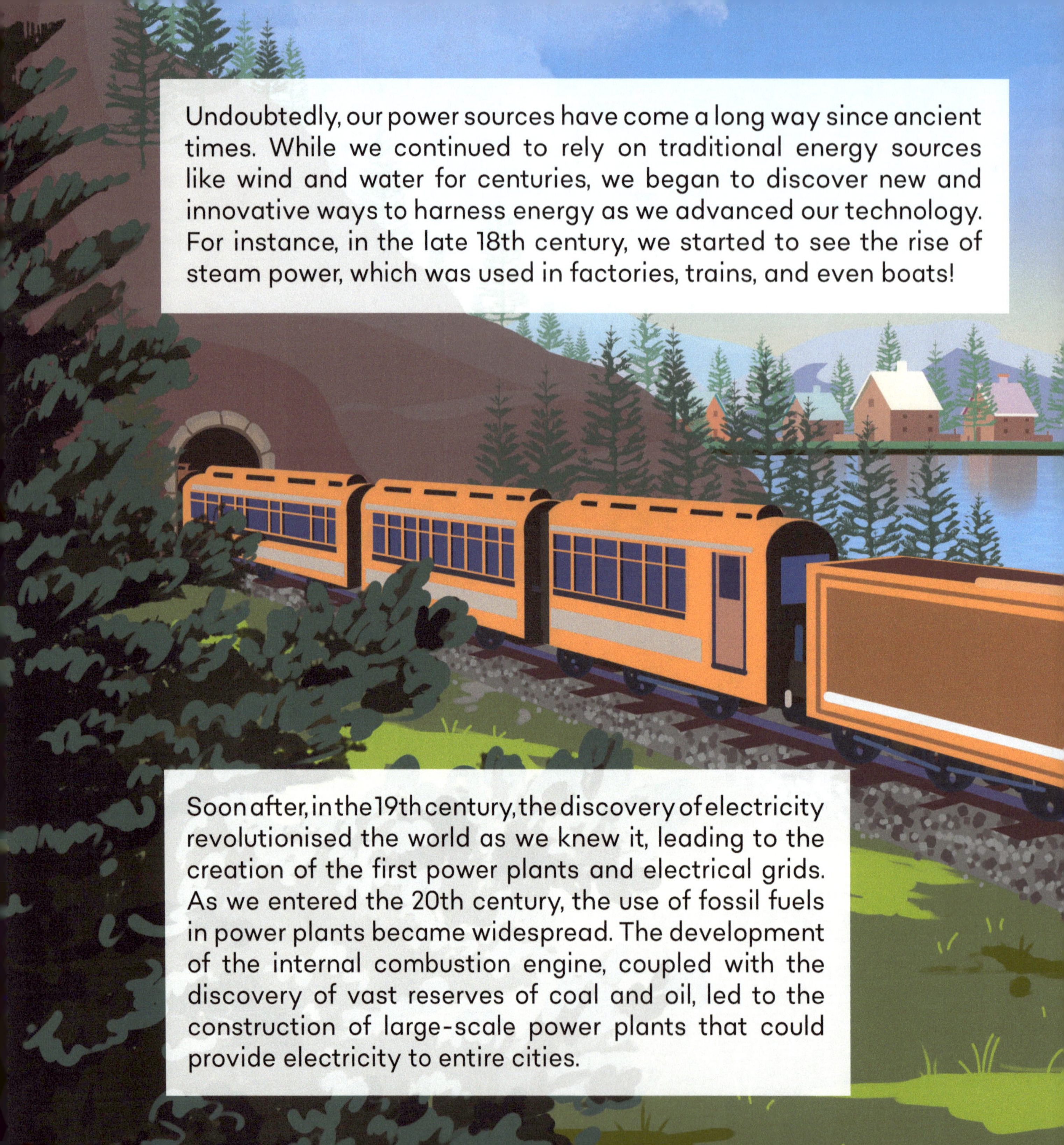

Undoubtedly, our power sources have come a long way since ancient times. While we continued to rely on traditional energy sources like wind and water for centuries, we began to discover new and innovative ways to harness energy as we advanced our technology. For instance, in the late 18th century, we started to see the rise of steam power, which was used in factories, trains, and even boats!

Soon after, in the 19th century, the discovery of electricity revolutionised the world as we knew it, leading to the creation of the first power plants and electrical grids. As we entered the 20th century, the use of fossil fuels in power plants became widespread. The development of the internal combustion engine, coupled with the discovery of vast reserves of coal and oil, led to the construction of large-scale power plants that could provide electricity to entire cities.

These power plants transformed the way we live and work, making electricity available on demand and powering our homes, businesses, and industries.

Although, over the past few decades, there has been a growing awareness of the negative impacts that traditional energy sources like coal, oil, and natural gases have on the environment. As a result, we have started to shift our focus towards cleaner and more sustainable forms of energy.

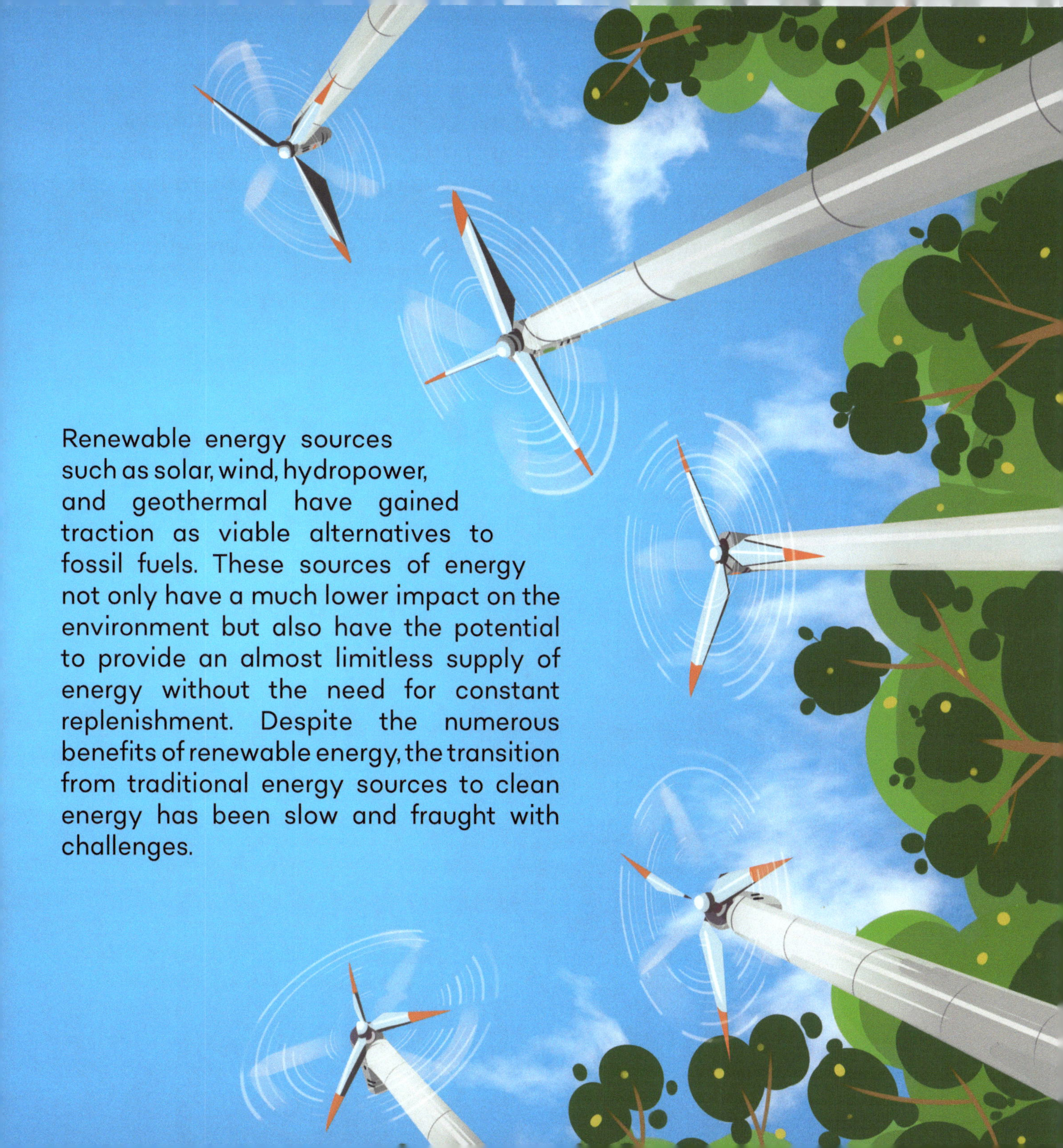

Renewable energy sources such as solar, wind, hydropower, and geothermal have gained traction as viable alternatives to fossil fuels. These sources of energy not only have a much lower impact on the environment but also have the potential to provide an almost limitless supply of energy without the need for constant replenishment. Despite the numerous benefits of renewable energy, the transition from traditional energy sources to clean energy has been slow and fraught with challenges.

But this trend is changing, and we are seeing a growing movement towards renewable energy sources. With the increasing demand for clean energy, energy engineers are more important than ever. These professionals are not only responsible for designing and building new systems to harness energy from renewable sources, but they also play a crucial role in ensuring that existing systems are optimised for maximum efficiency and sustainability.

That simply means that energy engineers work hard to make sure that we get more energy from these sources while also keeping their costs low for users. But that's not all – energy engineers also care about our planet and try to make sure that our power sources don't harm the environment too much.

This may have you wondering what it takes to become an energy engineer in our modern world. There are a few things to keep in mind. First, being an energy engineer requires plenty of maths, so it's important that you feel comfortable using calculations in your work. Additionally, knowledge of physics and chemistry can also be beneficial.

After establishing those foundations, you can then consider an advanced degree, as most energy engineers have at least a master's degree before practising in the field. Another important aspect of being an energy engineer is staying up-to-date with the latest advances in technology and renewable energy sources. This means keeping abreast of new developments, as well as staying connected with other professionals in the field.

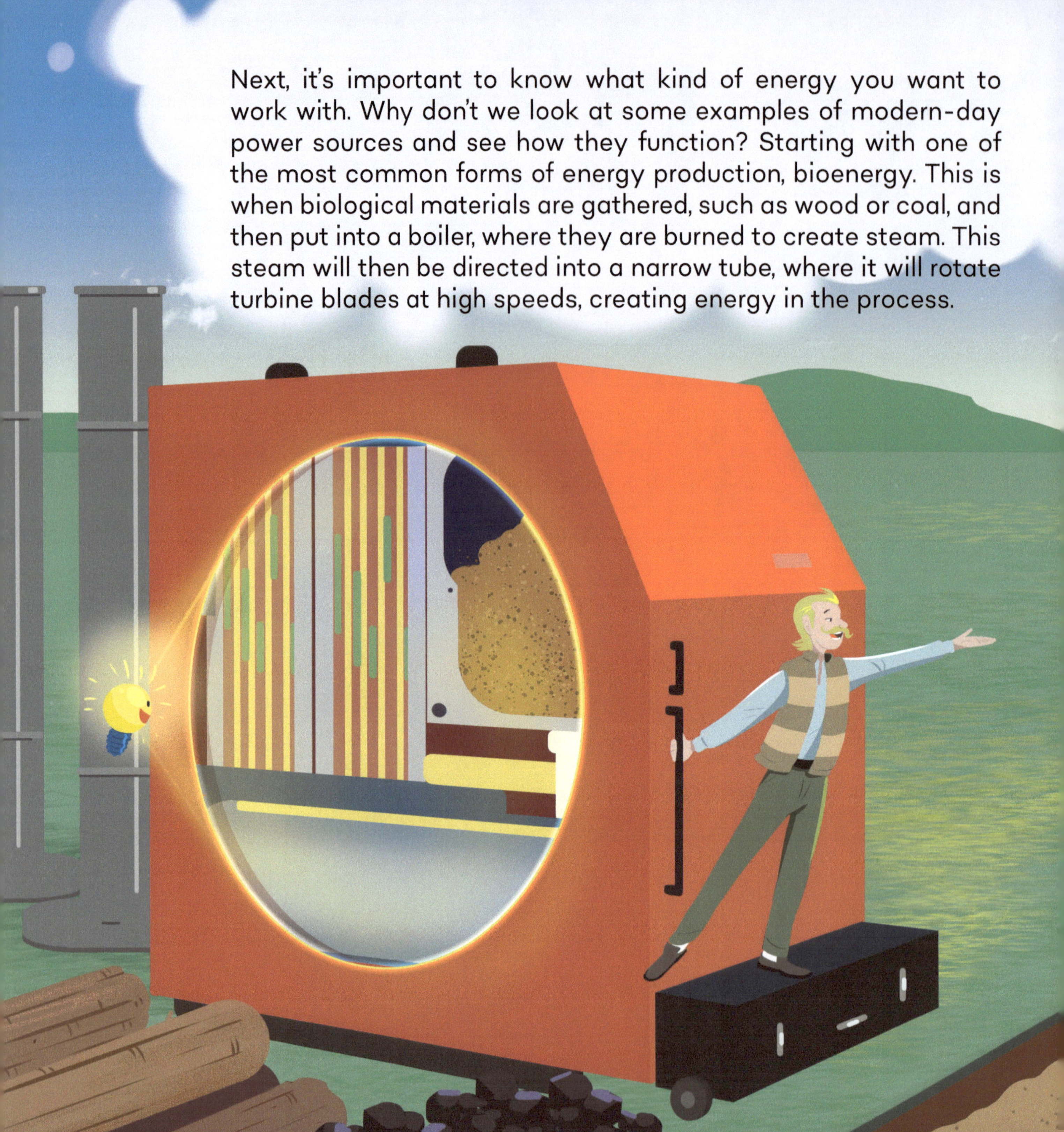

Next, it's important to know what kind of energy you want to work with. Why don't we look at some examples of modern-day power sources and see how they function? Starting with one of the most common forms of energy production, bioenergy. This is when biological materials are gathered, such as wood or coal, and then put into a boiler, where they are burned to create steam. This steam will then be directed into a narrow tube, where it will rotate turbine blades at high speeds, creating energy in the process.

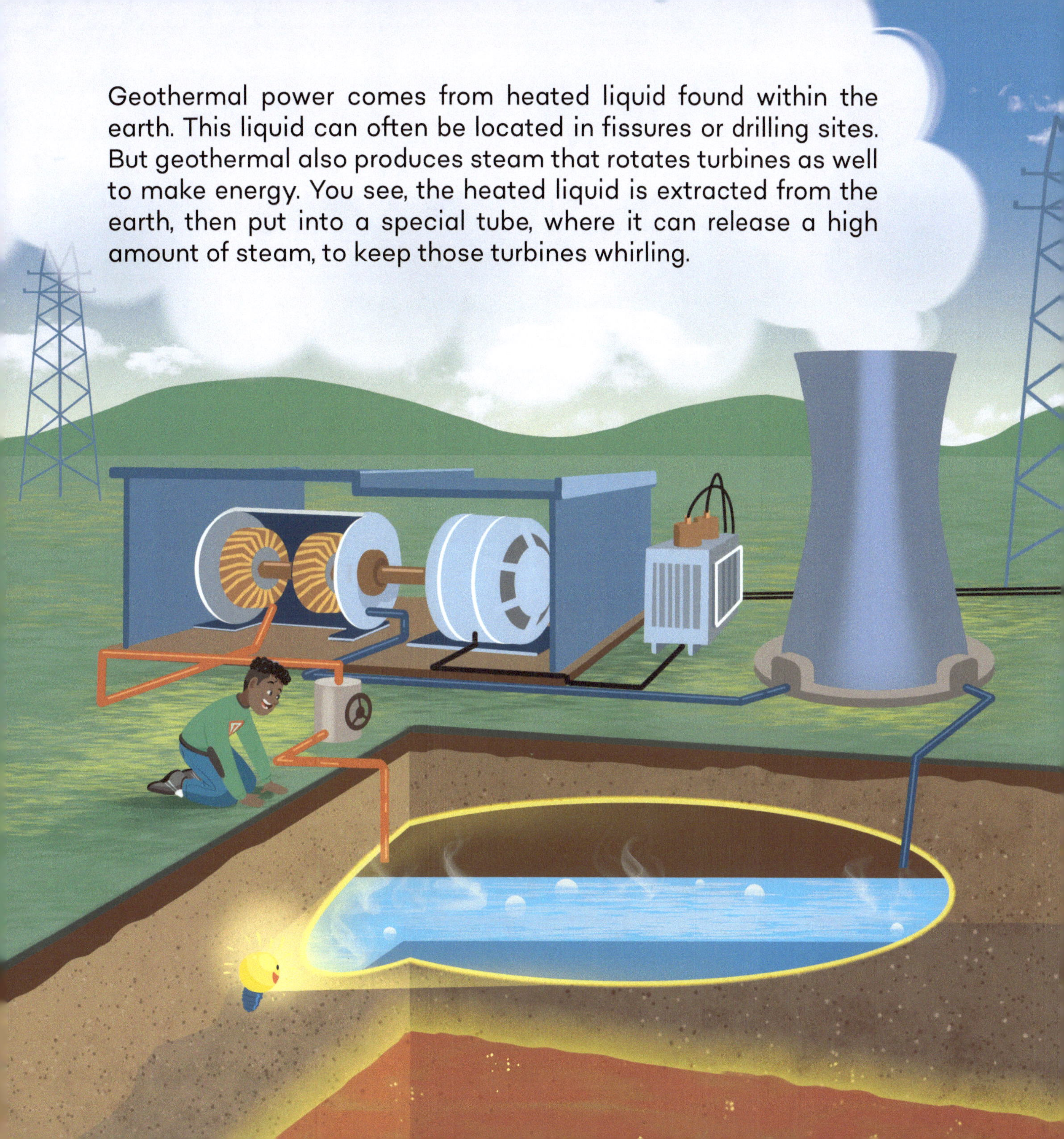

Geothermal power comes from heated liquid found within the earth. This liquid can often be located in fissures or drilling sites. But geothermal also produces steam that rotates turbines as well to make energy. You see, the heated liquid is extracted from the earth, then put into a special tube, where it can release a high amount of steam, to keep those turbines whirling.

Solar power has made a recent comeback as a reliable energy source. Modern solar panels are usually placed in areas where there is plenty of uninterrupted sunlight. They absorb rays from the sun, and then their PV cells convert that heat into electricity. After this, the energy is sent to a storage centre or straight to an appliance in need of power - right away!

Wind energy is very similar to the windmills we've seen in past civilisations. However, modern wind turbines are often much larger and placed in incredibly windy areas where they can keep spinning to produce energy. These turbines are also placed away from civilisation, so their source of power, the wind, won't be blocked!

Hydroelectric energy is created by rushing water that flows through pipes, where a water turbine is spun around, sending that collected energy to a generator. These power plants are often found in giant rivers, where an artificial dam has been created to control the flow of water and the output of the energy created.

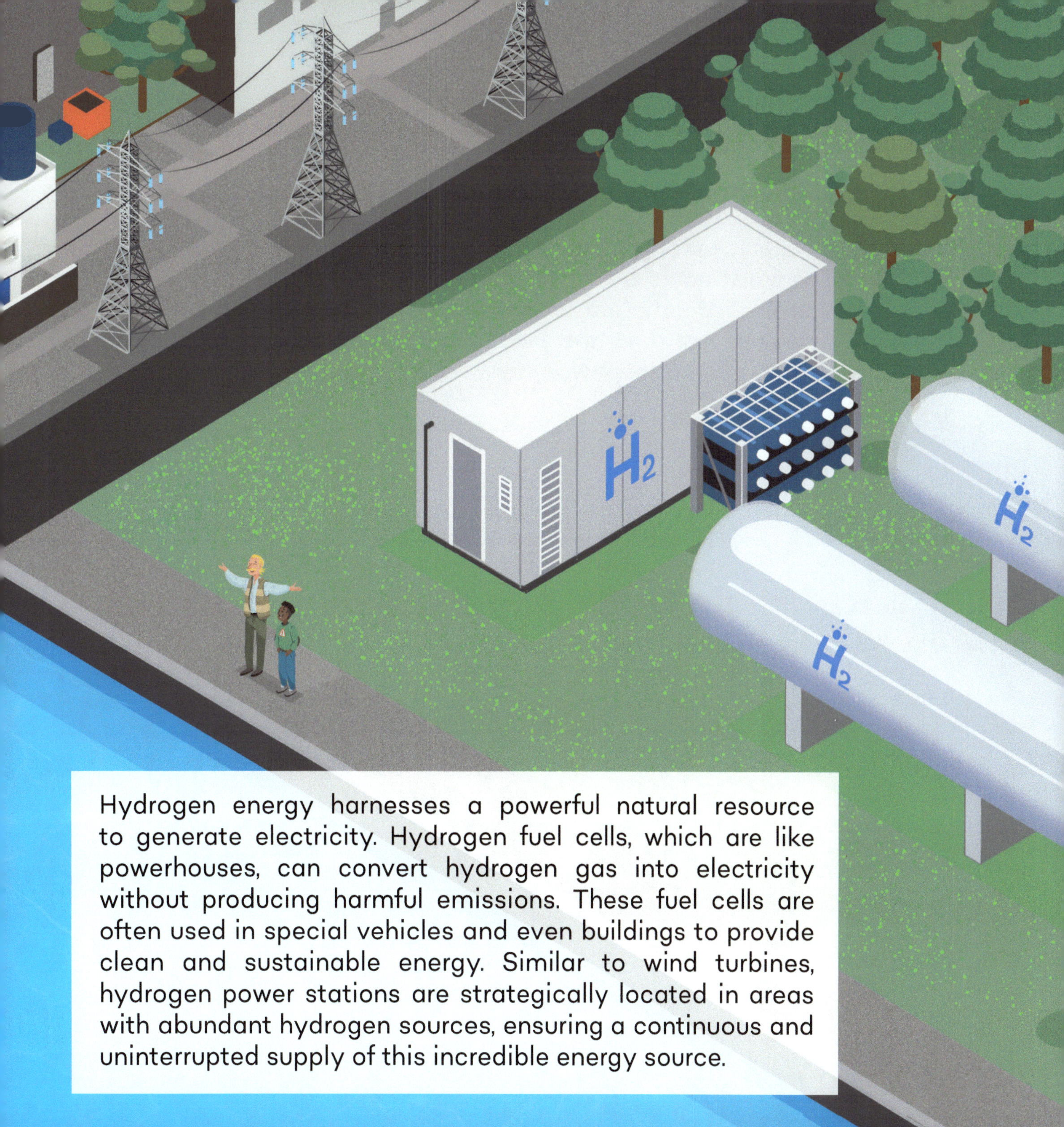

Hydrogen energy harnesses a powerful natural resource to generate electricity. Hydrogen fuel cells, which are like powerhouses, can convert hydrogen gas into electricity without producing harmful emissions. These fuel cells are often used in special vehicles and even buildings to provide clean and sustainable energy. Similar to wind turbines, hydrogen power stations are strategically located in areas with abundant hydrogen sources, ensuring a continuous and uninterrupted supply of this incredible energy source.

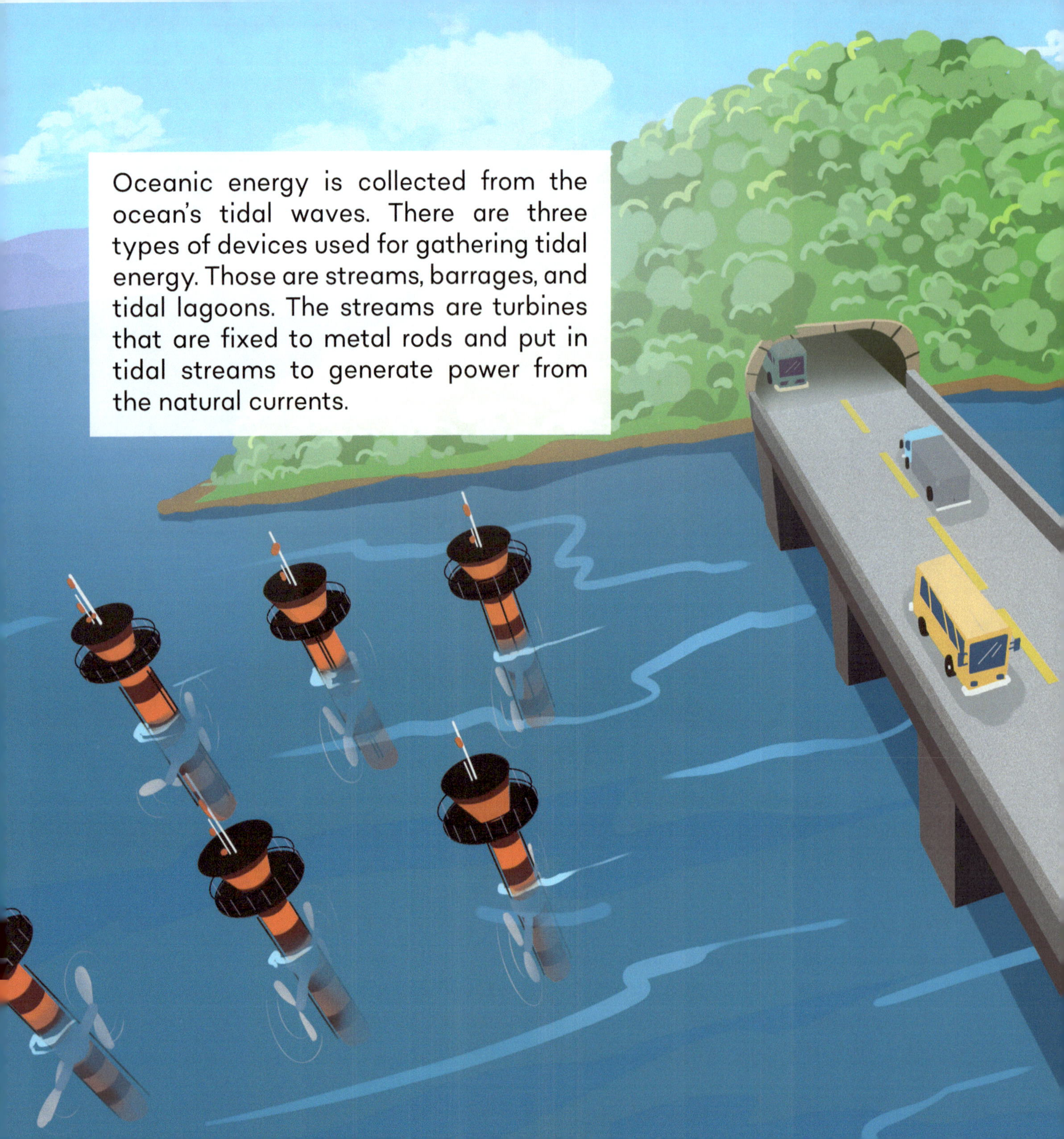

Oceanic energy is collected from the ocean's tidal waves. There are three types of devices used for gathering tidal energy. Those are streams, barrages, and tidal lagoons. The streams are turbines that are fixed to metal rods and put in tidal streams to generate power from the natural currents.

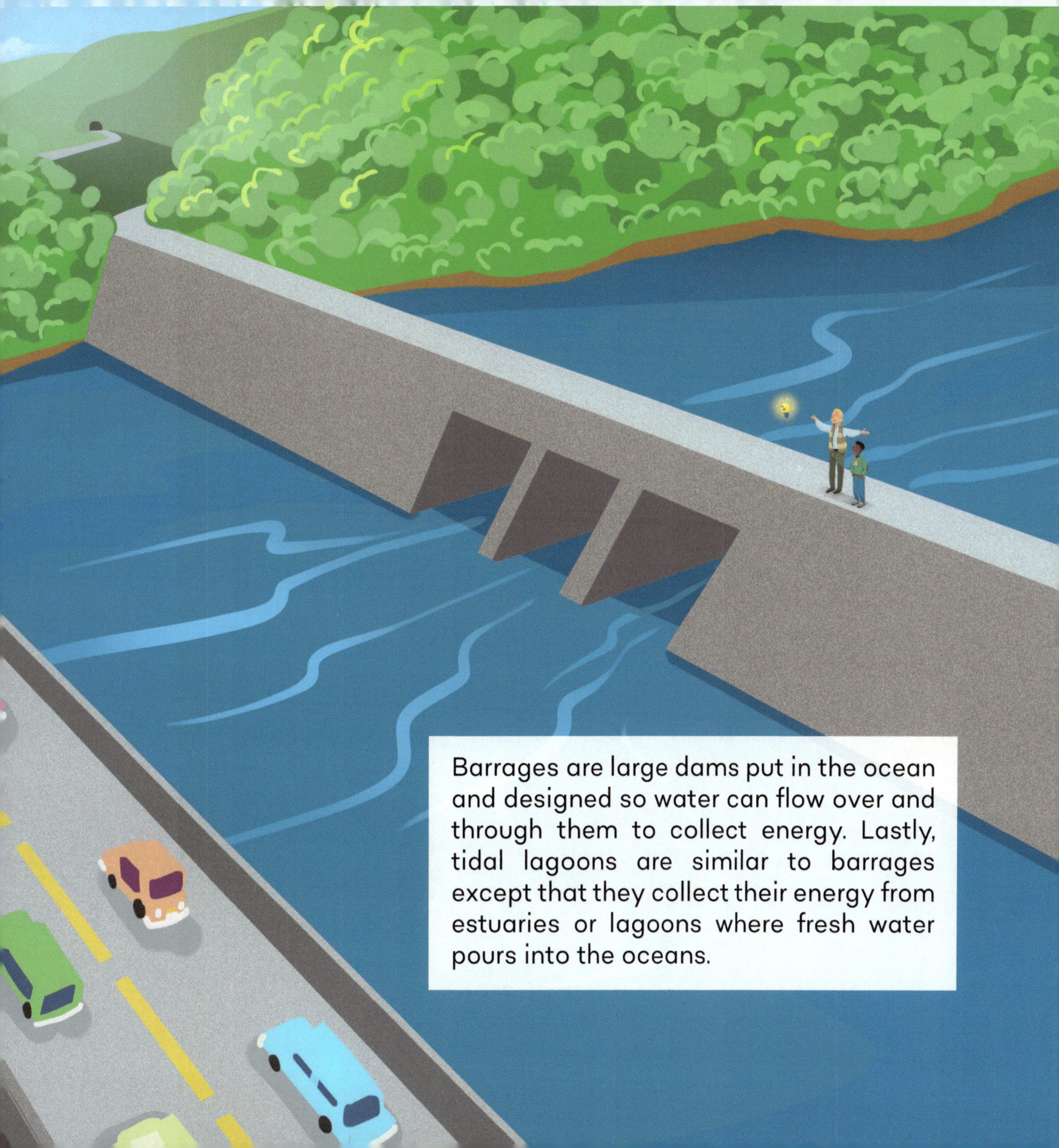

Barrages are large dams put in the ocean and designed so water can flow over and through them to collect energy. Lastly, tidal lagoons are similar to barrages except that they collect their energy from estuaries or lagoons where fresh water pours into the oceans.

As an energy engineer, you will play a critical role in creating a sustainable future for our planet. Your work will involve developing and improving systems that generate power with less impact on the environment. You may work with renewable energy sources like wind and solar or find ways to make traditional energy sources like oil and gas more efficient and eco-friendly.

Not only will your work as an energy engineer help protect our planet, but it can also be immensely rewarding. By finding ways to produce energy sustainably, you can help ensure that future generations will have access to clean and reliable power. You may also have the opportunity to work on groundbreaking technologies that could revolutionise the energy industry. As an energy engineer, you can truly make a difference and contribute to a better world for all.

My Inspiration

Shubhi Saxena
Founder, Unibino

As a parent in this ever-changing world, it can sometimes feel overwhelming when it comes to our children's futures. New technologies seem to be arising almost every day, and with so many innovations, it creates unique professions which many of us wouldn't have dreamed to be necessary only a few years ago. Which to me is a good thing. Because with so much variety, my children can have the opportunity to pick a career that will fit their personalities and build upon their strengths. As you may imagine, this desire within me to provide my children with the resources they needed to thrive, led me to search out books that would be easy enough for them to understand while teaching them about various professions.

Only, I found that these books were few and far between. Even if I could find a book about a certain profession geared towards young readers, I found them sparse inside and limited to only certain careers that may not fit my children's abilities. This is when I came up with the idea to write my own children's books, teaching them about all the various careers in the modern world. After months of researching different professions and learning more than I ever expected, I quickly realised this was going to be a bigger project than I first anticipated. I dove into the histories of these professions, discovering links to the past, and why these professions were now so important.

Ultimately my goal was to offer my children options, to show them that there is no one set path for everyone. But in this, I stumbled upon something bigger. I wanted to share this with future generations. To share with all children and parents about these careers, to help spark curiosity, and to instil a passion for the future. Everyone has special talents and abilities, and I hope that this series will be able to offer clarity and inspiration to children around the world. Because at the end of the day, it's never too early to start dreaming and never too late to take action. With this, I hope you enjoy this series and that your young ones become the best versions of themselves as they can achieve.